The Donkey Boy

by Doreen Harrison

WIPF & STOCK · Eugene, Oregon

Wipf and Stock Publishers
199 W 8th Ave, Suite 3
Eugene, OR 97401

The Donkey Boy
By Harrison, Doreen
Copyright©2015 Apostolos
ISBN 13: 978-1-5326-6936-1
Publication date 9/23/2018
Previously published by Apostolos, 2015

Dedicated to all the children in my life.

More Books from Doreen Harrison:

Jubilant Jeremy Johnson

Bouquet of Blessings

Garland of Grace

Coping with the Wobbles of Life

Contents

The Trouble with Rachel

Ben was eight years old and quite tall for his age, with a mop of long brown hair and the sort of constantly smiling face which always made you want to smile back. Ben lived with his mum, dad and baby sister Rachel in the little village of Bethsaida in Galilee. There had been two other brothers born between Ben and Rachel, but these had both become ill and died. There was a courtyard behind the house, with a well and a stable for the family donkey. Ben's father hired the donkey to people who had things to fetch or carry and he also hired Ben to be the donkey boy.

The donkey was trained to follow Ben and together they made a good team. But the donkey was sometimes lazy and then even a short errand might take all day. Ben never hit the donkey although he always carried a stick with him; it was just for effect, really. He wanted to look as efficient as possible. Usually he tried to coax the donkey to move more quickly by speaking gently to it or by giving it something special to eat. However, he was beginning to think that the donkey had grown wise to such treats and went slowly on purpose.

There were times when Ben did not want to work with the donkey. Like most boys his age, he wanted to climb the hills, catch fish in the lake and play games with his friends in the market. That was why Ben thought his name was very useful, for when his father shouted "Ben!", even if he shouted very loudly, it only took a fraction of a second to say, and so Ben could always pretend he hadn't heard. But the donkey knew his master's voice and he would begin to bray and make a fuss and so Ben always had to give in and answer his father's call.

Sometimes his father had a job for Ben and the donkey. There might be fish to collect for one of the market stalls. Then Ben would take the donkey down to the lake and the whole catch of silvery, slippery fish would be loaded into big baskets on the animal's back. Sometimes the fish were still wriggling and there would always be a terrible smell.

The fishermen enjoyed Ben's company and he liked to linger there by the water and the boats, but the stall holder wanted fresh fish and so Ben could never afford to waste too much time. Sometimes he had to collect olives from one of the small farms around the village. Ben always enjoyed it if he was asked to help to shake the ripe fruit from the trees. Ben liked to show off, and so he pushed the tree as hard as he could to make the fruit fall

Sometimes Ben's parents needed him to look after Rachel. That was one duty which Ben did not enjoy. He was not at all keen on babies, not even his own baby sister. Most people seemed to prefer babies to boys Ben's age and Rachel always got a lot of attention. Visitors would coo over Rachel and take no notice of Ben. They brought little presents for Rachel but never brought anything for Ben. When Ben complained about this, his mum said, "When you were a baby, Ben, everybody was kind to you. Now it's Rachel's turn." Ben decided that he simply did not want to be kind to Rachel. Actually, he was jealous of her, although he would not admit it. He would lean over her cot and pull a ferocious face; at which Rachel would giggle with delight! If Ben stuck his fingers in his ears and rolled his eyes, Rachel was even more delighted! There was no way in which Ben could let Rachel know what he really thought about her.

One afternoon, Ben had been left in charge of Rachel while his parents were busy in the courtyard. The donkey had kicked a hole in the stable wall and they were repairing it with mud and straw.

Ben would have enjoyed splashing around with the mud and the straw but his mother had been very determined that she was not going to allow him to make a mess. She said she thought that Rachel might even have a good effect on him. Ben looked at happy little Rachel with distaste. There was a pot of flowers on the table beside Rachel's cot. Someone had brought them, saying "flowers for your little flower." No one had taken any notice of Ben even when he fetched a pot for the flowers. Ben picked up the flowers, threw them on the floor and stamped on them. Rachel looked at him and laughed as Ben pulled one of his most unpleasant faces and added a growl, for extra effect; which made Rachel laugh even more. Ben was getting really annoyed. He picked up the pot and emptied the water into Rachel's cot. "There," he said, "flowers always need watering!"

Rachel went red in the face. She looked up at Ben and her mouth quivered for a moment before she began to yell. "Be quiet!" hissed Ben. But Rachel was really frightened and continued to scream. Ben pushed the flowers out of sight in a corner and put the pot back on a table. He tried to mop up the water from Rachel's cot, but the baby wouldn't let him come close to her and screamed even louder. Ben heard his mum and dad running across the courtyard, alarmed at Rachel's cries. He decided that the best thing for him to do was to run in the opposite direction; which he did.

Ben set off towards the river. He was not allowed to go there on his own, so he reckoned no one would look for him down there. He could still hear Rachel screaming and his dad shouting, "Ben come back at once!" Even the donkey was joining in the noise, because Ben had gone off without him.

Ben kept running. He slithered down the slope that led to the river. It was very deep, and could be dangerous for a boy by himself. That was why Ben was not allowed to go there unless an adult was with him. But Ben found that there were plenty of people around, because Wild John had just arrived. John was a travelling preacher, from the wilderness area of Palestine. He was called Wild John because of his clothes and his habits, but he was also known as John the Baptist. Whenever he came to a new place, John began to preach and warn the people that God wanted them to be clean from their sins. He would walk into the water, waist deep and challenge the people to come and join him, so that they could wash their sins away. Sometimes, when the people came out of the water, they would cheer or sing. Sometimes they cried. Ben's dad had taken him once to see what was going on. There had been a great crowd of people, listening to John. There were Bedouin from the desert, some Arab traders, local fishermen, and rich people from the nearby city. There were people from nearby villages, and a squad of Roman soldiers, watching to make sure John did not cause a riot.

There was just such a crowd around John today; and in the middle of all those people, Ben thought that he was well hidden. He looked around to see if he recognized anyone. There were some fishermen who knew him; in fact there were quite a lot of people from his own village and someone else who Ben knew very well. It was the carpenter from Nazareth. He had fitted new doors into Ben's house during the winter and he had become quite good friends with Ben. His name was Jesus. Ben tried to catch his eye, but Jesus did not seem to see him.

Ben saw Jesus step into the river and wade out to join John. The two men spent some time talking, and then Ben watched as John took Jesus by the shoulders and baptized him. He ducked Jesus right under the water, and then lifted him up again, just as he had done with so many other people. But this time was different.

Suddenly a beam of light blazed down on Jesus' head, and in the beam of light there was something like a white dove which stretched its wings over Jesus. And there was a voice, loud as thunder, "This is my son, the one I love. I am pleased with you." It was as if time stood still. For a brief moment the crowd, the sounds of the river, the birds, the scent of hay and flowers, all the colours around that place, everything seemed to be on hold. Everyone's attention was fixed on the light, the voice and on Jesus himself.

As Jesus shook the water from his head and his beard the people began to talk again, and someone else waded out to John to be baptized. Ben was amazed. He suddenly realized that this carpenter from Nazareth was a most unusual person. Jesus climbed up the river bank and stood beside Ben. He smiled at him. "Sometimes water feels cold," he said, "especially if you are a baby, like your sister Rachel." "He knows all about me," thought Ben, but aloud, he said, "I didn't mean to hurt her!" "Then perhaps you should tell her so," said Jesus.

As Ben made his way home, he thought about the voice in the beam of light. "This is my son – I am pleased with him!" He wondered if his dad could say that about him. Probably not, decided Ben. Just around the corner he met his dad with the donkey. They were coming to look for him.

Ben came straight to the point. "Dad," he said, "I poured the water on Rachel and I'm very sorry." "So you should be," said his dad, as he lifted Ben onto the donkey's back. When they got home, Rachel was really pleased to see Ben, and Ben realized that he was pleased to see Rachel too. "Sorry, Rachel," he said and this time he gave her his largest and sweetest smile and Rachel smiled back.

Delicious Dates

Ben's donkey was clever. It knew that big baskets on its back were followed by food baskets at its front and that the way to exchange one for the other was to follow Ben closely and carefully. The donkey had programmed itself to follow Ben. The boy in front and the donkey behind were a familiar sight in the town where they lived.

One day there was a load of dates to deliver to a man in Capernaum. Ben put two baskets across the donkeys back and then packed each basket with dates. They were freshly picked, plump and juicy. Sticky, sweet and oh, so tempting. Ben licked the juice from his fingers. Who would miss one small bunch? But his father was watching him load the dates, so Ben put them all in the baskets and set off. The donkey followed him. All the way to Capernaum, Ben thought about the dates. His mum had made him a packed lunch, and as soon as he was out of sight of his house, he opened the parcel. There was a little loaf, still warm from the oven some dried fish, rather salty, and an orange. Ben ate everything and thought about dates. He drank some clear water from a spring on the hillside and thought about date syrup and date wine. He was hungry for dates.

He reached Capernaum and easily found the house where he was to deliver his load. The man who had ordered them, unpacked each basket, and turned them upside down to make sure that he got all the fruit. He scowled at Ben. "I know what boys are like," he said. "I hope you haven't eaten any of my dates" Ben scowled back. "I don't eat dates," he replied. This was quite true; he didn't get a chance to eat any.

The man turned away to get the money to pay for the dates, and as he did so, his arm knocked one small bunch of dates onto the floor. Ben picked it up, and then, while the man was still turning away, Ben put the bunch into one of the empty baskets and pulled the covering cloth over it. The man paid Ben and Ben turned back into the street with the donkey following close behind. Now he was a thief as well as a donkey boy, but who was to know?

Capernaum was crowded that day. As Ben and the donkey made their way through the streets, they were jostled and pushed. "I'll find a quiet place to eat those dates," thought Ben, "and then perhaps the crowds will have moved on and we can make an easier journey."

There was an open courtyard just ahead with some outside steps leading up to the rooftop A huddle of donkeys were tied to some hooks in the house wall and one hook had a rope hanging from it but no donkey on the end of the rope. So Ben put that spare rope round his donkey's neck, and unpacked his bunch of dates. They were warm and juice was oozing out of them. Ben climbed the steps up onto the roof of the house. He found a place where the wall made a patch of cool shade and settled down to enjoy the dates. They were absolutely delicious. He ate all those sweet, sticky dates, licking his fingers so that he did not miss a single drop of syrup. Then he made a neat pile of the date stones and began pinging them down onto the heads of the donkeys tied up below. After that he lay down on the flat roof and peered over the edge.

He had chosen a busy house for his date feast. The donkeys in the courtyard below belonged to people who were visiting the house. There were so many visitors that a lot of people couldn't get inside, and they were wedged into the window spaces and pushing around the door. Ben had one date stone left. He threw it onto the neck of a boy standing on the wall around the courtyard. The boy rubbed his neck and looked up. "What's going on?" shouted Ben. "It's Jesus—in there," replied the boy. "They've all come to see Jesus."

Ben decided to climb down and then wriggle his way through the crowd to see Jesus. But as he reached the top of the steps, his way was blocked by four men who were coming up onto the roof. They were hauling a stretcher bed up with them on which lay a crippled man. Ben knew he was crippled because his legs were twisted at a crazy angle.

"Here, boy," said one of the men. "Watch our friend, will you?" He pointed to the man on the stretcher. Ben sat down beside him. He felt rather shy. He didn't know how to talk to a cripple. However, the crippled man had plenty to say to Ben. "I've never been on a roof top before," he began. "It's strange up here, looking down on the rest of the town. It's so near to the sun."

"Down there!" and he pointed. "The sunshine gets mixed up with the shadows. I'm usually lying on my mat underneath the gateway on Straight Street. I can't see the sky, I see peoples' feet and sometimes I have to shout to keep the dogs away. My friends put me there because a lot of people come through the gate and some of them give me money."

"I don't like being a beggar! I think I would like to be a shoe maker. I've seen a lot of feet and I'm sure I could make the most comfortable sandals in the world!" Ben was enjoying this conversation.

The man continued, "I've got four good friends—Seth, Joel, Reuben and Mark—I've known them since I was your age. Every day they carry me to the gate and every night they carry me home. If my begging bowl is empty they put something in it for me."

The man continued to talk. "We were playing in the hills when I fell."

When I was about your age—just after my eighth birthday —I slipped and went over a cliff. I broke some bones in my back and I've never walked since. They carried me home then and they've been carrying me ever since." Ben looked across at the four men. Then he realized what they were doing. They had some tools with them and they were tearing up the roof. "You can't do that!" he shouted. "We have!" said one of the men in a matter of fact way. Ben saw that there was a great hole in the roof. The thatch, even some of the supporting beams, had been pulled away and dust rose in a fine cloud. "We've brought our friend to see Jesus," one of them explained. "We couldn't get through the door or the windows, so we'll try the roof instead!"

The four men lifted the stretcher and Ben noticed that a strong rope was fastened to each of the corners. They carried the stretcher to the hole in the roof, and then, with each rope looped over their hands, they began to lower the stretcher through the hole. Slowly and carefully they lowered the man on his stretcher bed down into the room below. Ben came across and leaned over the edge. There were a lot of people there, looking up and some of them were reaching up to steady the bed until, with a gentle thud, it reached the ground. It landed right in front of Jesus.

One of the four friends called down to Jesus. "Hey, Jesus! I'm Reuben and this man on the mat is Marcus. We've been friends since we were boys together. We heard about you, how you can heal people. We believe you can heal Marcus. We couldn't get in through the door."

Another man joined in. "I'm Joel," he said. "I'm a builder and I'll make sure the roof gets repaired. Please can you repair Marcus?"

Jesus knelt down beside Marcus. "Your friends have a lot of faith," he said. "Son, your sins are forgiven." Up on the roof, Seth, Reuben, Joel and Mark looked at each other. This was not what they had expected Jesus to say. Some other people were also taken aback by Jesus words. In the crowded room there were some teachers and lawyers. They began to argue, "this carpenter from Nazareth thinks he can forgive sins?" said one. "Does he think he is God?" asked another. There was a hubbub of angry voices. "Look at the mess!" said someone else. "Who gave these men permission to disturb our meeting?" Ben nearly fell through the hole; he was so upset at what was happening. Didn't any one care for Marcus, lying there in the middle of that angry crowd?

Mark on the roof felt the same. He shouted through the hole: "Be quiet! We want Jesus to help our friend." The crowd fell silent and Jesus stood up. He looked at Marcus and smiled. "Now then, "he said, "which is easier, to forgive sins or to cure paralyzed limbs? Yet I will show my authority as the son of God! My friend, get up, roll up your stretcher bed, and go home." Marcus looked at Jesus. Then he looked at his poor twisted legs. Then, with a broad smile, he sat up, and then stood up; and then as the crowd all around him all began to talk at once, he rolled up his bed and walked to the door.

The people crushed back to make room for him, and Seth, Reuben, Joel and Mark, ran down the roof steps to greet their friend.

Jesus looked up and winked at Ben. Ben went pink with pleasure. "That was a miracle!" he said. "I forgave his sins as well," replied Jesus. Ben said, in a little voice. "My sins are only small ones." Jesus waited. "It was just one measly bunch of dates," reasoned Ben. "Is that why you were hiding on the roof?" asked Jesus. "So no one would see you eating them?" Ben nodded. "What shall I do?" he asked. "You tell me," answered Jesus. Ben gave a big sigh. "I'll go and confess to the man who bought the dates. I'll tell him I took a bunch, and if he says he doesn't want to use our donkey again, I'll have to tell my dad as well. "

Jesus held out his arms and Ben sat with his feet dangling through the hole and jumped. Jesus caught him and set him safely down on the ground. Then Ben untied the donkey and together they went to confess.

The man was sitting on a stool in the doorway of his shop. Ben looked at him solemnly. "I stole a bunch of your dates," he said. "I am sorry." The man looked at Ben. "I'm sorry you had to steal them," he said. "I have two bushels of dates and I couldn't spare you just one little bunch. How selfish I am! Here, take a few more small bunches; now let's shake hands and forget about it." Ben and the man shook hands. Ben turned up the road which led to his village, with the donkey following close behind. It felt good to be forgiven; and it had been quite a day.

Mysterious Uncle Seth

Ben had never met his uncle Seth. Seth was his mother's brother and sometimes his mother would look at Ben and sigh, saying, "Ben, you look more like your Uncle Seth every day!" But then she would say, "I'm sorry, we mustn't talk about Uncle Seth!" Sometimes when his dad was working with Ben he would begin to say, "I remember one day when Seth…" and then he would stop, look confused, and continue, "But we don't talk about Uncle Seth." Ben's Nan was Uncle Seth's mother. So one day Ben asked her, "Nan, is Uncle Seth dead?" His Nan wiped a tear from her eye as she replied, "No, Ben, Uncle Seth isn't dead. But we don't ever talk about Uncle Seth." There was certainly a mystery about Uncle Seth.

Ben and the donkey had delivered a load of wool to a merchant in the market. Ben had helped the merchant unload the heavy fleeces and stack them at the back of his shop. The merchant had given him two copper coins for his help, and Ben tied up the donkey just outside the gate leading into the market square, and he was taking time to look around the stalls, to find a pretty present for his little sister Rachel.

The market was crowded that afternoon and Ben noticed that Jesus was strolling through the market with some of his disciples. He recognized Simon, the fisherman, and Andrew, who was Simon's brother. He also spotted Matthew – who had once been quite a wealthy man, a tax gatherer working for the Romans until the day when Jesus had said to him, "Follow me."

Matthew had stood up at once—leaving all the money bags and the official papers on his desk—and gone off with Jesus, just like that. Everybody had gossiped about it and Ben and his friends had acted out the events and added their own endings. They pretended that the Romans had run after Matthew and dragged him back. They pretended that they had been there at the time and scooped up all the tax money and then spent it on anything they wanted. Barnabas said that Jesus could have pointed at the Roman soldiers who were standing at the tax table—to protect Matthew from thieves—and turned them into lepers. Ben's friend Barnabas didn't like the Romans. But Ben knew that Jesus would never hurt anyone and he refused to allow that ending.

Ben thought about Barnabas. He wondered why Barnabas wanted to turn even a Roman into a leper. Lepers were dangerous. Even a leper's breath was enough to turn the person who breathed it into a leper! That was why a person who had leprosy had to leave his home and family and live out on the hills. The people who knew them and loved them were advised to forget all about them.

Ben found a stall full of baby clothes. He had never noticed what Rachel was wearing but he knew she was small and still a baby. He thought she was certain to need something to wear because his mother was always saying that she had never known a baby grow as quickly. The stall owner recognized Ben. "How is that little sister of yours?" she asked. Ben explained about the two copper coins and that he was looking for a present for Rachel.

"I've got just the thing!" said the lady and she showed Ben a tiny shawl, embroidered with roses. "Just two copper coins for this," she said, "and I'll add some pink ribbons as well. She's a lovely baby; it's a pity Seth can't see her!" Then she looked confused. "I forgot!" she explained. "We don't talk about Seth. Since he developed leprosy, we are supposed to forget all about him." Ben was horrified. So that was the mystery about Uncle Seth. He was a leper. He took the parcel, with the shawl and the ribbons and turned toward the gate, to get the donkey. He wanted to get home as quickly as possible and ask his mum if what he had just heard was true. But coming through the gate at that very moment was a leper. His face was bandaged, with spaces for eyes and nose. He had bandages on his arms, too; he was thin and his clothes were ragged. The people pressed away from him, scattering from the gate. Someone overturned a stall in their hurry to escape and all the people were screaming. Ben ran to where Jesus was standing; he felt safer near Jesus. The leper looked across the market square and then he began to run over to where Jesus was, shouting as he did so, "Jesus, Jesus, if you will, you can make me clean!" The leper fell on his knees right in front of Jesus.

Ben covered his mouth and his nose with his hands. He tried not to breathe, he knew all about the dangers of lepers' breath.

But Jesus was smiling, and put his hand on the man's shoulder. "Of course I will!" he said, "be clean!" The leper looked at Jesus and Ben looked at the leper. He noticed the skin under the loose bandages, which had been grey and scaly, beginning to change colour. It gradually became pink and smooth, and as the leper tore away the bandage from his face, Ben saw that his whole face was healthy; the scales of leprosy had completely gone. The leper ripped the bandages from his arms and there too the skin there was clean and whole. The man jumped to his feet, raising his arms over his head. "I'm clean!" he shouted, "Jesus has cured me!" He twirled round so everyone could see what had happened. Then he saw Ben. "Ben? Is it you? You look just like your mother! Do you know who I am?" Ben didn't hesitate, "Hello Uncle Seth!" he said; then he threw his arms around his long lost uncle.

There was great rejoicing at Ben's house that evening. All the relations came around, Ben's smiling mum made a huge supper to celebrate Uncle Seth's return. Rachel wore the new shawl, and looked very pretty, but all the attention was on Uncle Seth. This was a happy family once again – and all because of Jesus.

Sunday Special

Ben and his donkey were well known in all the towns and villages around Galilee. The donkey was strong and Ben was reliable, so many people hired them to fetch and carry all sorts of things. Ben knew everything that was happening in the region, and he took a particular interest in Jesus. He listened to him speaking in market places, beside village wells and on the hillsides. What Jesus said made sense. He explained about God in words which Ben could understand.

"Look at the flowers," said Jesus. "Poppies with red silk petals as soft as velvet, golden corn swaying in the breeze like the fringe on a king's cloak. Why, even King Solomon in all his glory was not dressed as beautifully as these flowers are! If God looks after the flowers so well, of course he will look after you. Did you ever see a sparrow with a begging bowl in its beak? God feeds the birds and God will also provide for your needs. God will take care of you and He wants you to take care of each other. Love your neighbour as much as you love yourself."

The only argument Ben had with what Jesus was teaching was when he talked about the Sabbath day. Jesus reminded the people that God wanted them to keep that day special. Sabbath day was synagogue day, but Ben did not enjoy going to the synagogue. The men and the boys who were twelve or over sat together, but Ben had to sit with the other children and the women. Ben thought that a donkey boy who was ten years old was quite equal to any ordinary twelve-year-old.

His dad had different thoughts. "You'll soon be old enough to join us," he said, "meanwhile, make the best of what you've got."

Ben considered what he had got. He had to sit with the other young boys and the women and the small children. The women talked, gossiping and giggling; and sometimes Ben's mother would hand Rachel over to him, so that she could concentrate on her friends' conversations. Rachel really was a pain. She wouldn't sit still, and she wouldn't be quiet. And once, when Ben was trying to make her behave, she bit him hard!

One Sabbath morning, Ben decided he needed a change, a space from duty and especially from Rachel. As soon as breakfast was over, he let himself out through the back gate and began to climb up the hill sloping away from the village. He had planned his route in the opposite direction from the Synagogue. He had packed some food in a small basket: honey cakes, a circle of sesame bread and a few grapes; and he was wearing a new white tunic, as if to celebrate his freedom. The sun was shining, skylarks were high in the blue sky and a family of rabbits watching him approach let him get so near before scampering away that he could have caught the babies by their fluffy tails. A large yellow and green lizard blinked at him from a rock beside the road. Then Ben heard the sound of hoofs: clip, clop, clip, clop. He turned, and saw their donkey, trotting as fast as it could to catch him up. It had seen Ben leave by the back of the house and since it was its duty to go along with its master, it had broken its rope and followed after him. Ben scowled at the donkey, waving his arms to scare it off; but he couldn't shout in case someone, late on their way to Synagogue service, heard him

The donkey did not frighten easily. Ben picked up a stone and threw it at the donkey. For a moment the animal hesitated, it lowered its head and flattened its ears to its skull; but it still came on after Ben. When Ben broke into a run, the donkey started to gallop; he just could not get rid of him! Up ahead, Ben noticed that there was a bend in the road, and charging round the bend, he jumped off the path and slithered down a muddy bank into the middle of a thicket of thorny bushes, out of breath and out of sight.

On the pathway above he heard the sound of the donkey, trotting briskly up the path.

Ben waited until he could no longer hear the sound of the donkey's hoofs, and then he tried to creep out of his hiding place. However, he was stuck! Some of the sharp thorns had meshed into the material of his new silk tunic, and as he struggled to get free, the material tore and tangled some more. The harder he pulled, the tighter he was fastened in. Ben was frightened now. There were lions in those hills, scorpions and snakes. He had dropped his food basket in his haste to get down the hill and escape from the donkey. If the wild animals didn't get him he would probably starve to death. People did not travel on the Sabbath day; he might be there all night in the dark with danger all around. How he wished he had gone to the Synagogue—the safe synagogue—with his family and even with Rachel to look after.

Ben remembered what Jesus had said once about coping with difficulties. "Pray," Jesus had advised, "for your heavenly Father is always listening for you and he will always help you."

Ben knew that he was in big trouble right then, and so he cleared his throat and looked up at the small area of sky visible through the thorny branches. He kept his eyes open; he was too frightened to close them.

"Excuse me, God," he said. "I know I should be in the Synagogue, and you know I'm not. I wish I was! Please, God, I am in a mess. Can you help me?" He thought for a moment, and then he added, "Amen."

When he had finished praying, Ben heard a familiar sound in the distance; it was the sound of a donkey's hoofs! His donkey was coming back to find him. Ben heard the donkey stop on the path above, and then slither down the bank towards him. A flurry of stones fell all around him and then a long, velvety muzzle pushed through the thorny branches. His donkey had found him!

Now, the donkey was so used to being behind Ben, that once it had discovered where he was, it ambled around the back; Ben could hear it chewing the thicket behind him. Donkeys have strong mouths. They can munch thistles and thorns like young boys eat bread and butter. The thicket thorns were thick and long and so the donkey opened its mouth wide and took a huge bite. It bit through the thorns, into Ben's tunic and also chewed a little piece of Ben! "Ow!" he shrieked, and shot out of the thicket. He landed with a thud on his hands and knees. The donkey pushed through after him, still chewing. It was in its right position now, with Ben in front. Ben got to his feet. He brushed himself down. The new tunic was tattered and torn but at least he was free.

He set off home at once, very much shaken by his experience. Once he had tied the donkey securely in the courtyard and given it fresh water and a pile of hay, he changed out of his torn clothes and went immediately to the Synagogue. As he got there, the service was just finishing and Ben saw his friend John rushing over to meet him.

"Where were you, Ben?" he asked. "You missed all the excitement!" John pointed to a man called Caleb, who was standing in the doorway of the Synagogue, surrounded by a crowd of people. The last time Ben had seen Caleb, he had been a bent old man with a withered arm hanging uselessly by his side. Today, Caleb had two straight strong arms and looked about twenty years younger. John explained what had happened. "Right in the middle of the service, Jesus stood up and told Caleb to come to the front. He told Caleb to stretch out his arm and when he did so—oh, Ben it was amazing—his arm suddenly straightened in front of our eyes! Why, look at Caleb for yourself. And, oh, Ben—you missed it."

Ben was thoughtful. "I'll *definitely* be here next week," he said to himself. "I prefer Synagogue excitement to a thorn bush any day."

When Ben got home, there was excitement of a different kind. His mother was cross when she saw his torn tunic. Rachel had screamed all through the synagogue service and now she kept being sick. His father was upset that the donkey had been out on a day which was intended as a rest for animals as well as for humans. So Ben was scolded and sent to bed without any supper. Still, he didn't mind too much; after all, it was better than spending a night all alone in a thorny thicket and what was more, God had answered his prayers.

At Sea in a Storm

Ben and the donkey often worked down on the fish quay. The fishermen were friendly to Ben. They always spoke to him, and if their nets dredged up an unusual shell or stone, they would put it on one side to give to Ben. He had quite a collection, which he kept on a ledge near the ceiling in the kitchen, out of Rachel's reach.

Ben wanted to go out in a fishing boat and catch fish by moonlight, and when his day's work was over, he would hang around the boats, hoping someone would invite him on board. However, fishing is hard work, and no one had time or space to take along a spare crew boy like Ben. One evening, as he hung around the boat that belonged to some of Jesus friends, he noticed that there was a pile of ropes and covers near the prow, and a space between that looked just as deep as he was wide. No one was watching, so he climbed over the edge of the boat and snuggled into the space. It was a perfect fit His knees bent under his chin as he curled into the curve of the ropes. The waves rocked the boat, very gently, and made a splashing sound against the side. There was a smell of tar, seaweed, sunshine and fish. Ben closed his eyes. "I'm a fisherman," he imagined. "I'm right out in the middle of the lake. There's a big splashing ahead of us. Is it a giant fish? Is it like the one that got Jonah? It's seen me, that big fish. It recognises me, Ben, the big fisherman. It's swimming as fast as it can, to escape, but I am just as fast. It won't get away." He imagined the chase, the speed of the boat through the waves, the fury of the fish; he was really dreaming now. Curled up in the boat, he was fast asleep.

When the men came to push the boat out, Ben didn't wake up. Jesus was with the fishermen, and he settled down in the stern of the boat and he fell asleep. The four fishermen spoke to each other in low voices and rowed steadily, so that Jesus could rest easily. Of course, they did not know Ben was on board.

Sometimes the wind rushed down the valleys in the hills around Lake Galilee which acted like funnels, sending great gusts over the water, churning the sea into waves and tossing the boats violently up and down. That night, one such storm blew up and the tempest hurled itself against the fishing boat until the water began to swamp it.

Ben woke up with a start as the sea hit the boat, and clutched the sides as it went deep down into the trough of the next wave and shuddered up the crest of the next one; leaving him violently sick. Ben saw a huge wall of green water rapidly approaching the little boat. The force of that wave knocked him right onto the floor and he was in danger of drowning. "Help!" he shouted, but no one could hear him above the howling of the wind. The fishermen were just as afraid as Ben. They were used to the sudden changes in the weather, but they had never seen a storm as dangerous as this. One of them lurched over to the back of the boat to shake Jesus awake. "We are sinking!" he yelled. Jesus calmly stood up, lifted his arms as if he was going to bless the sea, and he spoke to the wind and waves saying, "Be quiet!"

Immediately, as if a giant hand had smoothed them out, the waves stopped. The boat stopped rocking and the water lapped gently against the sides of the boat.

Ben thought, "Perhaps I'm dead. Is that why it's so quiet?" However, he could feel the coldness of his wet clothes and when he stood up, he could see the fishermen and Jesus still with him. Ben was so relieved that he began to cry. Jesus reached over and lifted him out of the space in the front of the boat. Ben clung to him. "I thought I was dead," he sobbed. "And I wonder what your mother is thinking about you?" said Jesus. Ben realised how anxious his mother, dad and Rachel would be, and this time he cried for them, not for himself.

The fishermen had no difficulty rowing the boat over the calm sea. As they made for the shore, Ben could see his dad and the donkey standing on the beach. "We were so worried about you," said his dad, "and the donkey went missing as well. Someone came up from the fish quay, and told us our donkey was down there, making a dreadful fuss at the edge of the water. So we guessed you were on one of the boats. Oh, Ben, we were so anxious!"

"I'm sorry," said Ben, and he cried again, because he couldn't find words to say what he really felt.

Later, however, when he was telling the family about the storm and how Jesus made it stop by saying, "Be quiet!" he found just the words he needed. "It was as if Jesus owned the sea," he said. "The winds and waves obeyed him as if they belonged to him." Outside the donkey was making snuffling noises into its straw. Ben continued, "And the donkey obeys me because it belongs to me." His mother laughed. She said, "Now that would be marvellous! Donkeys which obey their owners and children who obey their parents! Now off to bed with you young man, you've had a busy day!"

Pigs in a Panic

Ben was a tidy, polite donkey boy and he seldom made a mistake. The donkey had programmed itself to follow Ben; he would lead and the donkey would follow. It was a wise old animal which saved its energy by letting Ben do all the planning. The donkey was quite dilapidated: its hoofs were dull and cracked, its teeth were broken and yellow, and there were bald patches on its back. Even its ears drooped wearily on each side of its face. "You are absolutely ugly!" remarked Ben one day. "What must people think, when they see a smart boy like me, followed by an old wreck like you!"

He walked round the donkey, considering ways of improving its appearance. The donkey twitched nervously, and closed its eyes. "It's your colour," decided Ben. "You are just the colour of dust. You are a dusty, dilapidated old donkey. Well, I can improve that." By the side of the well in the courtyard were several jars full of the lotions, oils and dyes which his mother used when she was weaving cloth. She kept them there because some of them had to be mixed with water, and they were out of Rachel's way. Ben picked up one of the jars. "Here we are," he said, "I think this is oil to make your hair shine," and he tipped it over the donkeys back. "Oh dear," thought Ben. He had chosen the wrong jar. It was not oil at all, but a jar of dye, and before his horrified eyes the donkey had turned bright purple!

When Ben's mother and father found out they were not amused, although Rachel thought it was hilarious. His father decided that he would prefer Ben to be out of reach for the rest of the day, and arranged for Uncle Reuben, who lived next door, to take Ben with him on a business trip across the lake to Gadarene.

His uncle looked sternly at Ben, but as they left the house he winked at him and the boy brightened up. He could hear the donkey creating a fuss in the courtyard because it couldn't follow Ben, and he really felt sorry for what he had done. All the same, he was very excited at the thought of crossing the lake, and he enjoyed Uncle Reuben's company. Jesus and some of his friends were on the same boat. Jesus saw Ben and waved to him.

Soon they reached the other side. There was a sandy beach which quickly became rocky, and rose steeply into a cliff with caves. Some of the caves were blocked with stones because they had been used as graves. Suddenly out of this grave yard jumped a fierce, wild-looking man with nails like claws. He was dirty, too, and dressed in only a few tattered rags. Round his wrists and ankles were broken chains and there was blood smeared over his face and shoulders. The people who had just got off the boat were terrified; they clustered together, and Ben hid behind Uncle Reuben.

The wild man ran straight to Jesus, grovelling on the sand at his feet. He threw handfuls of sand around as he shrieked, "What have I to do with you, Jesus, son of the most high God?" His voice echoed round the cliffs and the echo copied his voice, "Jesus, son of the most high God!"

Jesus looked calmly at the man. "What is your name?" he asked. The wild man stretched his arms high in the air. "I am Legion" he yelled. "Legion, legion," the echo repeated. There was a herd of pigs feeding on top of the cliff. The yell disturbed them. The man was on his knees again, scrabbling in the sand. "Tell these demons to go into the pigs," he pleaded. Jesus lifted his hands in a gesture of authority. The man gave a scream—those pigs were completely unsettled now—"Go!" said Jesus.

At once the pigs went mad and threw themselves over the cliff edge and down onto the beach. It was a dreadful sight.

Ben buried his face against Uncle Reuben; he didn't want to see what had just happened to the pigs. Everyone was silent: such a silence! After that, small sounds broke into the silence; the lapping of the waves and a startled seagull. Ben could hear the thudding of his own heart, as Uncle Reuben led him away up the path from the beach and into the town. Down below everyone seemed to be talking at once.

Later, when Uncle Reuben had finished his work in the town, they climbed back onto the beach. Someone had cleared the mess of pigs away and there, sitting under the cliff, was Jesus and with him was the wild man. Only he wasn't wild any more, he looked quiet and was wearing a clean tunic instead of old rags. Ben only recognised him because his hair was still long and tangled. Ben would like to have heard what Jesus was saying to the man, but Uncle Reuben led him onto the boat for the trip back home.

Ben rehearsed the events of the day in his mind. He was glad that the donkey had stayed at home, or it might have joined the pigs under the cliff. He thought about Jesus who could stop storms in human hearts as well as storms at sea. He thought of the large herd of pigs and how one wild man had been more important to Jesus than all of them.

He also thought about the donkey; who would it look after a day under the scrubbing brush?

All Things Bright and Beautiful

Ben's donkey was now a delicate shade of pink, with orange hoofs. Ben's father made it clear that he preferred brown donkeys and so Ben was being extra good and helpful, hoping that this would encourage his dad to forgive him about the dye. He patted the donkey; even the animal looked at him reproachfully. Ben was just hoping that the donkey would forgive him as well when his mother called him. "Ben," she said, "I want you to take some oranges over to Mary and Jairus' house in Capernaum. Their daughter Anna is sick, and maybe the fruit will help her to get her strength back."

The pink donkey looked quite attractive with the basket of bright oranges balanced on his back and his matching orange hoofs. As they reached the market place, people stared at the donkey, pointing to his gaudy hoofs and giggling at his pink hair. The donkey did not appreciate the attention it was receiving, and twitched nervously. He stayed so close to Ben that his hot breath tickled Ben's neck.

Jesus was in the market place too with his friends. As usual, people were crowding around, listening to him. Ben has just stopped to listen when someone came pushing past them through the crowd. It was Jairus, one of the rulers of the synagogue. He was an important man, and usually looked very smart and dignified. But today he was dishevelled and obviously upset, for Ben could see that he was crying. He fell on his knees in front of Jesus in the dust and dirt of the busy road.

"Jesus! Oh Jesus!" he pleaded, "I need your help!"

"My daughter is so ill," Jairus continued, "and they say she is going to die. Please will you come and make her well? No one else can help, only you can heal her." Jesus helped Jairus to his feet. "Of course I'll come," he said.

Jesus began to walk towards the house on the hill above the market place, where Jairus lived and the crowd went with them. Ben followed, trying to keep as close as possible to Jesus. He didn't want to miss out on this healing; and besides, he had a basket of oranges to deliver to Jairus. "A get well present from me," thought Ben.

Someone touched his arm and a quiet voice said, "Excuse me, may I pass you?" It was an old lady. She looked pale and thin and was leaning heavily on a stick. Ben stood on one side to let her come through, and she smiled her thanks at him; then reaching out her hand she touched the hem of Jesus coat. Ben saw what happened next: immediately, the lady's white, weary face flushed pink and she stood up straight, no longer needing the support of her stick. Even her wispy hair seemed to have new life in it. Jesus turned around "Who touched me?" he asked. The lady looked up at Jesus. "I did," she explained. "For twelve years I've gone from one doctor to another and none of them have helped me. Then I heard about you Jesus, and I thought to myself, that if I could only touch you, I would be sure to feel better." She gave a skip and a jump. "Now look at me!" she said as Jesus smiled. "Your faith has healed you," he said, "Now, go and live a healthy life." The lady twirled round, so that she could share her new found health with the people and as she did so, she noticed the donkey. She began to laugh; she laughed and laughed until tears ran down her cheeks!

The donkey lowered its head and gnashed its teeth at Ben—no one likes being laughed at, not even a donkey—Ben scowled back at the donkey. "Stupid thing," he said. Then he put his arms around its pink neck and gave it a big hug.

Jesus continued up the road with Jairus, but some of the people who came running down the hill towards them were obviously agitated. These men were servants from Jairus' house, and they spoke sadly to him. "Master, do not trouble the teacher Jesus to come any further. Your daughter is dead. While you were away, she sighed, closed her eyes and died." Jesus put his hand on Jairus' arm. "She is not dead," he said, "she is only sleeping."

They continued up the hill, but most of the crowd stayed behind. They did not want to intrude, for they did not want to be part of the disappointment which Jairus would feel when he reached home and found that indeed his daughter had indeed died. Some of Jesus' friends went with him, though, and Ben and his donkey followed as well. "After all," thought Ben, "I do have some oranges to deliver."

Outside the house, a group of official mourners had already arrived. They were wailing, playing sorrowful tunes on flutes and weeping. Jesus raised his voice above the noise: "she is not dead," he said, "but only asleep." Jesus and Jairus went into the house as Ben waited outside. He lifted the basket of oranges and placed it on the ground beside his colourful donkey. He thought that perhaps he might give it to one of the servants, but all the doors were firmly shut. He had just decided to leave the gift at the side of the front door, when that door was flung open and a little girl appeared. "Anna!" cried Ben.

The flute players stopped their music, and the astonished mourners stopped wailing. The general cry arose from the lips of the crowd: "It's a miracle!" they said, as Anna danced into the courtyard.

As the crowd began to dance and sing with the little girl, a servant came out and spoke to the man standing nearest to Ben. "Jesus went into the girl's room where she was lying dead, pale and still. Jesus took her by the hand, and said, 'little girl, it's time to wake up.'" The servant paused for breath, then she finished her story, "and the girl came back to life!"

Jairus' daughter, now joined by her mum and dad, continued to dance and play with the sunlight on her laughing face, alive and glowing. Ben stepped forward and held out the basket of oranges. Anna looked at the basket of fruit, then she looked at Ben, and then she noticed the donkey. She laughed, pointed to the colourful donkey and laughed even more. Everyone joined in. The donkey seemed to know that being bright and beautiful was right on occasions like this and he joined in with raucous braying.

The servants came out with trays of sweet biscuits and glasses of grape juice and Jairus' wife Mary cut the oranges into slices to share with the people. Someone wove a garland of red geraniums and slung it round the donkey's neck, to add colour to the celebrations. While they were all laughing and singing for joy, Jesus and his friends quietly left. The official mourners packed their things and went back to the town as the happy family went inside to rejoice together. Ben was thoughtful as he led the donkey down the hill. He had witnessed a great power in his friend Jesus, and he needed space to think about the events of this amazing day.

The Swallow's Song

On account of an accident with some purple dye, the dilapidated donkey now looked so exotic that many more people wanted to hire it; especially as the deal included Ben as donkey boy. Ben was smart and strong and the donkey and he made a good team.

Just before Passover, they were hired to deliver some special oil for the festival to a Rabbi in Jerusalem. Ben's father was going as well, and it was decided they would stay for the celebrations with some of their relatives who lived in a house which was built right into the city wall.

Ben found the journey to Jerusalem very interesting, although the many miles of walking made his legs ache and the donkey rather ill tempered. All three of them were glad when they had delivered the oil and finally settled in for the night at their relatives' house. The next morning, Ben got up early to explore his surroundings. Not only was the house built into the city wall of Jerusalem, but part of the roof was actually the top of the city wall, which people could walk on. There were steps from the roof which led down into an alley on the other side of the wall. Opposite this alley—outside the city wall—was a rocky cliff, with caves that looked like eye sockets. Ben found out later that the hill was called "the place of the skull", because that is what it looked like. At the bottom of the cliff there was a beautiful garden with a wall around it and a gate to keep it private. It was quite a contrast to the ugly cliff-face above it. Inside this garden was a new tomb—no one had yet been buried in it—which had been carved out of the solid rock of the cliff. One morning at breakfast, Ben's aunt told him that the garden belonged to someone named Joseph, from Arimathea, and that one day, Joseph would be buried in the cave there.

It was the day before the Sabbath and still quite early, and Ben's dad said he could take some time to go into Jerusalem and see the sights.

Jerusalem was a big, bustling city, crowded with the people who had come from far and near for the Passover celebrations. The place sizzled with colour, scents and sounds. Along one of the streets, people were lined up as if they were waiting for a procession to pass by, and Ben joined them. "Here they come!" someone shouted, and four fully armed Roman soldiers marched into the street. Ben craned his neck for a better view; and what he saw behind the soldiers made Ben's heart stop; it was absolutely horrific. Three men staggered up the road, bleeding from whip lashes all across their backs. Their faces were grey with pain and fatigue, and they were dragging great pieces of wood, each one the beam of a crucifix. The men were going to be crucified.

Ben stared at the men, slowly realising that one of them was Jesus, the carpenter from Nazareth. Jesus wore a crown made of thick thorns which had been violently jammed onto his head, tearing the skin and causing the blood to run down his face. Ben simply could not believe that Jesus was about to be crucified. He stepped into the road, in front of the Roman soldiers and shrieked, "Stop! "You've made a mistake!" A woman in the crowd quickly caught hold of Ben and pulled him back, out of the way of the soldiers. She muffled his mouth with her hand. "Quiet!" she hissed. "Never interfere with the Romans – they might kill you too!"

Ben stood in silence as the Romans and their victims moved slowly out of sight. Then, with tears streaming down his cheeks, he walked slowly home. He found his donkey tied beside the house and clung tightly to its pink neck; crying until he had no energy to cry any more. Up on the hill—the one that looked like a skull—the Romans hammered nails into Jesus' hands and feet and slung him up on a cross.

When Jesus eventually died, the sky became dark, even though it was only three in the afternoon. Ben climbed up onto the roof of the house and watched the friends of Jesus bringing his dead body down into the beautiful garden and placing it in Joseph's tomb. He watched as they rolled a great stone over the entrance. Roman soldiers came to seal the stone with their official seal. Ben felt as if the light had gone out of the world.

On Saturday morning, Ben climbed down into the alley and went to the garden gate. It was shut and he looked over it towards the tomb. Swallows were skimming nearby, and roses were rambling over the rough rocks of the cliff. The scene was one of beauty and life; but uppermost in Ben's mind was the fact that inside the garden—buried in a tomb—was the body of Jesus. Ben felt tears brimming into his eyes again. He wiped them away and as he did so he heard a faint, cheeping sound. He looked down, and there, near his feet, was a wounded swallow. Its wing feathers were bent and broken and there was fresh blood on its body. Some animal must have caught it and tossed it away. Ben gently picked it up. It was too weak to struggle, so he carefully tried to straighten the wing as he stroked its tiny head. Beside the garden gate was a small gap in the wall left by fallen stones. This space was narrow, but Ben lined it with moss and carefully placed the swallow inside. He knew the bird was dying. All through the day he kept returning to see if it was still alive. By night fall he knew that the bird was not likely to see another dawn.

On Sunday morning, Ben got up while it was still dark. He climbed down into the alley to check on his rescued bird. Puffs of morning mist curled all over the ground like smoke and the grass was damp with dew.

When Ben reached the garden gate, he saw that it was open. The hollow place where he had placed the bird was empty. Cautiously Ben stepped into the garden. It was still not dawn, but the garden was full of light.

The tomb in the garden had been opened, for the stone had been rolled away. A glorious golden light filled the garden, and Ben saw that it was streaming out of the cave. Slowly, a man emerged from the tomb and smiled at Ben. It was Jesus! As the man held his hand up to the light, Ben could see his wounded swallow, perched on his open palm. Yet it was no longer wounded and broken, but full of life as it sang a song of joy. As Ben watched, Jesus raised his hand and the swallow soared high into the sky, as if he had been set free from a cage. Just then the sun began to rise and all the birds in Jerusalem began to sing.

"I thought you were dead," Ben said to Jesus. "Well, I was dead Ben, but now I am alive forever," said Jesus. "Ben, always remember this. No one can ever kill God."

Ben ran back to the alley, climbed the wall with the agility of a monkey and burst into the house to share the news. He wanted everyone to know that Jesus had come back to life again.

This is an unusual book. Here is the last page, but it is not the end of the story, but the beginning, as Ben discovered in the months and years ahead.

www.ingramcontent.com/pod-product-compliance
Lightning Source LLC
Chambersburg PA
CBHW071353130626
46556CB00005B/2171